If Only Donkeys Could Talk

Sam's Christmas Question

By Joye Thackston
and Kim Dulak
Illustrated by Emily Kozora
Editor Adria Schmedthorst

In loving memory of Remington Bird

"Mom, look at the church! There is a donkey in the baby Jesus' house." Sam pointed out the car window, an excited look on his face. "It looks like grandpa's donkey." He turned back to look at his mom.

"But Mom, why is a donkey standing there?" Sam was on his way to play school on a cold December day. Christmas was just around the corner and Sam was really hoping for snow.

"It's not a real donkey, Sam. Now put on your hat. We're almost there. I have a lot to do at work and we're running late." Sam's mom gave him a quick smile, taking one hand off the wheel to give him her hurry up sign.

"But Mom," Sam said, "What about the donkey?" Sam stuck his nose to the window trying to catch sight of the church again.

"Sam, your hat!" his mom reminded him again.

Nativity Scene

As they pulled into the school circle, Sam crushed his hat onto his head, but his mind was still on the donkey. "If only donkeys could talk," Sam thought, "then it could tell me why it was at the baby Jesus' house."

Sam's teacher was at the door to greet the kids. Sam really liked Mrs. Dulak. She was always very nice and Sam thought that Mrs. Dulak knew just about everything.

"Mrs. Dulak will know why the donkey was at the baby Jesus' house," Sam thought. "Mrs. Dulak, I saw a donkey on the way to school. It was at the church," Sam said, stopping on his way in the door.

"That's nice, Sam. Now, put up your coat and take a seat. We have a lot planned today and the clock is ticking," Mrs. Dulak said with a smile.

"But, Mrs. Dulak!" Sam cried.

Mrs. Dulak pointed to Sam's chair and raised one eyebrow. Sam knew it was time to take a seat.

Mrs. Dulak

Sitting in his chair with his chin resting on the table, he thought again, "If only donkeys could talk."

At lunch Sam sat by his best friend, Isaac. Sam remembered, "Isaac is older than I am. He always has his birthday first. He knows lots of things." Sam leaned forward and whispered, "Isaac, guess what I saw on the way to school this morning? I saw a donkey by the baby Jesus house at the church. Do you know why a donkey was there?"

"How should I know?" Isaac answered with a shrug. "We don't go to church there. Hurry up and eat so that we will have more time to play ball."

Sam threw his hands in the air. "If only donkeys could talk!" he said.

"What did you say Sam?" Isaac had a funny look on his face.

"Oh, nothing," Sam said. Let's go."

Play Ball

On the way home from play school that day, Sam and his mom passed by the church again. The Christmas lights lit up the little house.

"Mom look, there is the donkey." Sam pointed, bouncing up and down in his seat.

"Sam, shh. I'm on the phone with a client. We'll be home in just a few minutes."

Sam sat back in his seat, folding his arms across his chest. "If only donkeys could talk," he mumbled to himself.

That night, Sam had to go to bed early because his mother said they had an early morning the next day. "No sleeping late on Saturday, Sam, I have a surprise for you in the morning," his mom said with a smile as she tucked the covers around him.

"But Mom, what about the donkey?"

"Sam, sleep." Sam's mom leaned over and gave him a soft kiss right on the tip of his nose before turning out the light. Sam drifted off to sleep whispering under his breath, "If only donkeys could talk." All night Sam dreamed of donkeys talking.

Cardinal Lights

The next morning when Grandpa opened his door, Sam knew just what his surprise was.

"Sam wake up. Your mother is working today, so we get to spend the day together." His grandpa clapped his hands as he left the room. Sam got dressed as fast as he could and then ran to the kitchen where his grandpa was sitting down drinking coffee and rubbing his knee.

"What's the matter, Paw-Paw?" Paw-Paw was what Sam called his Grandpa.

His grandpa pointed to the barometer on the wall and shook his finger at it. "Every time that goes up my knee gives me trouble." Sam thought a minute, then pushed a chair against the wall and climbed up into it. Sam took the barometer off of the wall and looked at it for just a second. Smiling at his grandpa, he turned it upside down and hung it back up.

"Sam, what are you doing?" his grandpa asked.

"I'm fixing your knee, Paw-Paw," Sam said as he jumped down from the chair.

Stunned, Grandpa began to laugh. "I wish I'd thought of that sooner," he said as he gave Sam a big hug.

Grandpa's Barometer

"Well Sam, what would you like to do today?" he asked with a smile.

"Let's go to your house out at the farm. I want to see Balaam, your donkey," Sam answered quickly.

His grandpa grinned, "I was guessing that was exactly what you might like to do."

"Paw-Paw," Sam said, "I dreamed about talking donkeys all night. I really wish they could talk."

"Well, maybe they do, to each other," Grandpa said.

"No, to us Paw-Paw," Sam laughed.

His grandpa thought for a minute and then said, "I guess if God wanted them to, they could."

"Has Balaam ever talked to you?" Sam asked with a frown.

"No Sam, but maybe he's never has had anything to tell me," Grandpa answered.

Grandpa's Red Pickup

Sam thought for a minute then asked, "Paw-Paw, why did you name your donkey Balaam?"

"Your mother said you had some questions." Grandpa smiled at Sam. "We can answer them at the farm. Let's get going. I want to read something to you."

Sam loved to ride in Grandpa's old red pick-up truck, because he got to buckle up in the front seat. "Paw-Paw, can we please back-up Hard Bargain Mountain," he asked excitedly. "I see it!" Sam pointed and bounced up and down.

Grandpa pulled off the farm road and onto a dirt road running beside it and turned the pick-up around so that he could back-up the mountain like Sam asked. Sam turned so that he could see in the mirror. "Tell me the story again, Grandpa," he said.

"Well, Sam, a long time ago the fuel would drain to the back of the carburetors. The only way we could get to the top was to back up old Hard Bargain. Our cars didn't have the fancy carburetors that are on the cars today. Kinda the same theory you used to fix the barometer, Sam. Your grandmother and I backed up this mountain many times," Grandpa gave Sam a smile.

"Now it's our time, right, Paw-Paw?" Sam smiled back.

Hard Bargain Mountain

Arriving at the farmhouse, Grandpa and Sam went in the back door. Grandpa's Bible was always open on the kitchen table. Picking up the Bible, Grandpa said, "This is what I wanted to show you, Sam."

"I've seen your Bible, Paw-Paw," Sam said.

"I know, Sam, but I want to read you a story. This story has a donkey in it," Grandpa whispered as if it was a secret.

Grandpa turned to Numbers 22:28 and began to read:

> *Then the Lord opened the mouth of the donkey and she said to Balaam, "What have I done to you that you have struck me these three times?"*

Grandpa told Sam how the donkey saw the angel that Balaam, his master, had not seen. Balaam was not obeying God and the angel was sent to redirect his path.

"I guess the donkey was smarter than Balaam right, Paw-Paw?" Sam asked.

"Maybe so, Sam." Grandpa smiled. "That's how my donkey got his name. He reminded me of the story of Balaam," he explained. "But, why have you been so interested in donkeys lately?" Grandpa patted the chair next to him and Sam sat down.

Grandpa's Bible

Sam looked at his grandpa. "I saw a donkey like Balaam by the little Jesus house at the church," he said. "Was there a donkey with baby Jesus the day he was born?"

"Oh, you mean the nativity scene." Sam's grandpa leaned back thinking. "Sam, you remember how Mary rode a donkey to Bethlehem and there was no room for them at the inn?" he asked. Sam shook his head yes and his Grandpa smiled. "I'm sure they kept the donkey close by," his grandpa explained.

Sam thought for a minute. "If God wanted that donkey to talk he could have told a lot of stories about baby Jesus, right Paw-Paw?"

"I'm sure of it, Sam," his grandpa said and patted him on the back.

"Can we see Balaam now, Paw-Paw?" Sam asked eagerly.

"Go jump in the pick-up and we'll go find him." Grandpa smiled when Sam jumped up with a whoop of excitement.

Mary and Joseph

After driving around in the pasture, Sam spotted Balaam by a grove of trees. Grandpa parked the pick-up and they walked toward Balaam. But, each time they would start to get close, the donkey would move away again.

"What is Balaam doing, Paw-Paw?" Sam asked. "Do you think he sees an angel?"

Grandpa laughed, "Maybe so, let's just follow him and see." Finally, Balaam stopped and let Sam and his grandpa walk over to him.

"Well, Balaam," Sam's grandpa said, "Are you going to talk to Sam?" Balaam let out a loud "Hee-haw!" then turned his head toward the tree he was standing beside.

"Well, Sam, I think he is trying to tell us this is the perfect Christmas tree," Sam's grandpa said with a smile.

"What do you mean, Paw-Paw?" Sam asked. His eyes were bright with excitement.

"This is the surprise your mother was telling you about," his grandpa answered, giving the tree a pat. "We're going to get the Christmas tree today."

Perfect Christmas Tree

Sam jumped up and down. "You mean that we get to have a real Christmas tree this year?" he squealed.

"We sure do," his grandpa said with a grin. "And Balaam found it for us." After Grandpa loaded the tree in the back of the pickup, they headed back to Sam's house. As they backed up Hard Bargain Mountain for the second time that day, Sam was silent for about ten minutes. Grandpa was just starting to think that Sam might have fallen asleep when Sam said quietly, "Paw-Paw, you were right."

"About what, Sam?" Grandpa asked, glancing over at Sam.

"God can make a donkey talk if he wants to," Sam said in a sure voice. "Paw-Paw?" Sam continued.

"Yes, Sam," Grandpa said.

Sam's face was serious. "I think we need to change Balaam's name."

"Why, Sam?" Grandpa asked.

"Balaam in the story was mean and not very smart." Sam answered, nodding to himself. He thought for a moment before continuing, "Let's change his name to Special. OK, Paw-Paw?"

"That sounds good to me Sam. From now on his name will be Special." Grandpa reached over and ruffled Sam's hair. "Balaam was a special donkey,"

Grandpa thought. "But Sam, is an even more special kid."

Special

THE END

WestBow Press books may be ordered through booksellers or by contacting:

WestBow Press
A Division of Thomas Nelson & Zondervan
1663 Liberty Drive
Bloomington, IN 47403
www.westbowpress.com
1 (866) 928-1240

ISBN: 978-1-5127-6186-3 (sc)
ISBN: 978-1-5127-6187-0 (e)

Library of Congress Control Number: 2016917800

Print information available on the last page.

WestBow Press rev. date: 10/28/2016

WESTBOW
PRESS®
A DIVISION OF THOMAS NELSON
& ZONDERVAN

CPSIA information can be obtained
at www.ICGtesting.com
Printed in the USA
LVOW05s1917211116
513975LV00003B/3/P